Boxing Day

A ROMANCE NOVELETTE

Catina Noble

crowecreations.ca

Boxing Day © 2024 Catina Noble
First Crowe Creations Print Publication November 2024

Author photo © Anne-Marie Binda
Cover photo © from iStock. Credit: Harahliad ID:1185474729
Cover Design © 2024 Crowe Creations
Interior design by Crowe Creations
Text set in Times New Roman; headings set in Courier New

Crowe Creations ISBN: 978-1-998831-39-5

Mona, Cheryl and Diane. Till we meet again.

When you least expect it.

1

THAT NIGHT, WHEN TED CAME HOME, Becca once again tried to talk to him about their marriage. He said he didn't want to talk about it so she made what turned out to be the crucial mistake of suggesting they attend couple counseling. To her astonishment, Ted angrily picked up her favorite childhood mug and with glaring eyes, whipped it in her direction. She managed to duck, but it missed her head by mere inches and hit the ivory-colored kitchen wall—that she'd just painted last month—where it smashed into pieces. Becca's eyes widened in disbelief. That was when she knew her marriage was over for good.

She turned to walk away but he grabbed her by the wrist—hard—and it hurt. Her squeals didn't make him let go. She tried pulling away, repeating that he was hurting her. Still, he refused to let go.

He kept his grip firm until their son, eight-year-old Jeremy, showed up in the kitchen, asking what was going on because he'd heard a loud noise and was scared.

Unable to contain them, Becca's tears fell. There was no turning back. Their lives would never be the same.

Ted and Becca had shared twelve years together. Four years into their marriage, Jeremy had arrived and he was the best thing that had ever happened to her. She was a mother first and that

1

meant protecting Jeremy at all costs. So they left Ted.

Ted had always been a casual drinker but as Jeremy grew into a toddler, Ted's drinking—along with his attitude—had become worse. He started doing as little as possible around the house and with the family. She was appalled at the amount of beer he was consuming every night. It just kept increasing. No matter how much Becca tried talking to him, he hadn't listened and constantly told her she was being dramatic.

What had Becca expected? Ted was a lawyer so "it was normal to have a couple of beers now and then, wasn't it?" The problem was, though, Ted wasn't having just a couple of drinks, he was becoming a full-blown alcoholic—a functioning one— but still… To add to all that, instead of coming home after work to have supper as a family, Ted was stopping in at local bars to have "a couple of drinks" with friends.

She tried to give him slack. She knew being a lawyer wasn't easy, but enough was enough. It seemed the more she tried to help and understand him, the angrier he became. Becca knew the signs. Her own mother had been an alcoholic but had managed to hold down a job and run a tight ship at home. As a child, Becca obviously didn't have a choice, but things were different now. She was a grown woman with a family of her own. Over her dead body would she subject her son, Jeremy, to the same cycle of abuse she herself had endured for too many years to count. She would not let that happen.

Ted had always been a good father, had never raised his voice at Jeremy. At least there had been that. He'd never been physically violent toward Becca either. Until the mug incident.

So why was Becca replaying this in her mind now? Four years later? She stared at the phone in her hand, finding it hard to comprehend the call she had just received.

2

NUMBNESS TURNED TO UPSET. Upset turned to disbelief.

Chad?

The phone call had been from Shawn, Chad's best friend.

Strange how, when things ended, you thought of past relationships. For some reason, it had always been like that for Becca. She wondered if it was like that for everybody. But thinking about past relationships and mistakes was not going to make her feel any better. She was thirty-five and needed to get her life in order.

She had set the phone down and told herself: *I don't need a man. I am a strong independent woman.* And she had tried to shake off the call even though all she wanted to do was curl up into a ball and cry.

Love sucks.

She replayed the conversation.

"Becca. It's Shawn."

"Hey. How are things? How's Zoey doing?"

"She's good. Baby is fine." He hesitated. "Actually, I'm calling about Chad." Another pause, then, "He isn't who you think he is."

Becca had been at work. She had no idea where this conversation was going but she wanted to make sure none of the other staff or any of the youth overheard, so at those words, she'd walked into her office, made sure the door was closed, and sat down. Shawn's voice had sounded different, strained.

"I'm sorry," she said. "I don't really know what you're talking about. Can you be more specific?" She took a deep breath and waited.

"He's cheating on you."

She heard him inhale. He probably wanted this conversation over just as much as she did. Her heart missed a beat. A strange statement. She took the bait anyway. "How do you know? I mean do you have any actual proof? I don't understand where this is going." She wished he would just spit the words out and get everything into the open.

"I know he's cheating on you because, well… It's with me. We've been sleeping together for the last several months. I kept hoping he'd tell you but he said he had an image to maintain and refused to break it off with you. Anyway, it's up to you what you want to do with this information but I had to let you know."

And with that, Shawn hung up without giving Becca the chance to ask any more questions.

***

Becca didn't leave her office for the rest of the afternoon. She stayed behind closed doors playing catch-up on paperwork. At least that's what she'd attempted to do. Her thoughts kept reverting back to all the times she and Chad had shared over the last few months, playing them over and over again in her mind. One by one, she pulled them out to examine them. In each one, they'd shared a laugh, and a great time. They'd spent the night together several times. The only thing that stood out was that Chad had always seemed preoccupied with his phone. She'd even made a comment about it once but his reply quickly brushed her off, stating it was work related. He worked at a youth center, just like she did, but a different one. Becca was the

Executive Director at her center but she wasn't on the phone nearly half as much as Chad was.

***

Becca's son, Jeremy, would be turning eleven right after Christmas. In fact, his birthday was on New Year's Day. Becca always believed that made him extra special. Jeremy really was a great kid. He always took things in stride. He hardly threw tantrums, for which Becca was grateful.

Ted had become the best father ever. He always made sure he was there for Jeremy and had shouldered a lot more responsibility. Becca was the community supervisor for underprivileged youth which meant she was always busy. She had her regular hours but when working with young people, it was inevitable for the unexpected to pop up. Sometimes teens were in abusive relationships, or their parents were neglectful. Being caught shoplifting was not uncommon. Attempted suicide was also on the long list. From one day to the next, Becca never knew what was going to happen and that was the best part of her job. When things came up and she needed someone to take Jeremy, Ted was always there and she was most appreciative of that. Obviously, she knew that Jeremy was also Ted's responsibility but he could have made things difficult for her if he'd wanted to. Ted gave her a decent amount for monthly child support and the payments came regularly.

***

Becca's hairdresser, Tammy, sensed that something was off but didn't press for details. She just chatted away about her upcoming trip. She was going to Cambodia in two months and was obviously thrilled. This meant the countdown was already on. Becca listened as Tammy rattled off about what she needed to bring, the climate and the difference in currency. Becca, who had barely taken in a word Tammy said, sighed deeply.

Tammy frowned. "Are you okay Becca? Did you get some

bad news or something?"

Becca shook her head. She needed to remain focused, stay in the present moment. Ruminating about her past wasn't going to do her any favors.

Becca handed Tammy a fifty dollar bill and walked away. The amount was always the same—thirty-eight dollars—but she always paid Tammy with a fifty. The rest was a tip.

The moment Becca got into the safety of her car, she let all the pent-up tears go. Who could blame her? She honestly thought Chad might have been *the* one. Boy, had she been wrong! Maybe she was meant to be alone for the rest of her life. *Maybe I'll collect cats after Jeremy moves out and be known as a cat lady.*

As she pulled into her own driveway on Holly Lane, she decided she was done with relationships. She had invested too much time and energy in Chad. She had been sure she was falling in love with him. What a waste.

No. She had to stop this line of thinking. She was over-reacting. It wasn't like they'd been together for years or anything. She was acting silly, really.

It's not your fault. It's not your fault. It's not your fault.

She would ask Chad to remove his few belongings while neither she nor Jeremy was home. The last thing she needed was to deal with him or for Jeremy to ask questions while Chad was packing up. At least she'd been smart enough to not let him move in with her. He'd been there every other weekend and sometimes one or two other nights during the week.

She thought about that for a moment. She'd been skeptical after Ted and was now patting herself on the back for acting on the intuition to take things slow. Thanks heavens for the little things.

***

Becca had met Chad two years after her divorce had been

finalized. He was six feet tall with long blond hair that he kept in a man bun, hazel eyes that, when he was in the right mood, reminded Becca of sunflowers. He was a little on the thin side, but not too much so. Ever since she was a little girl, Becca had always enjoyed sunflowers, thinking them unique compared with other flowers.

They'd met because of work. At the center where Chad worked, he did the same type of work as she did but more closely with youth who struggled with addictions. One day, Chad had stopped by Becca's center to check in on one of his young clients who had been released from the hospital the day before. After that, it seemed that he was stopping in more frequently. A lot more than he needed to. Finally one day, he asked her out for coffee and she agreed.

They had a great time and discovered they shared common interests although he'd never married and didn't have any children. Becca took things slowly. They had dated four months before she introduced Jeremy to Chad. The meeting had gone smoothly. Jeremy and Chad seemed to get along great.

Shortly after they started dating, Becca had a conversation with Chad about Jeremy already having a father, which meant Chad could just be himself. She told him he wasn't going to suddenly find his plate filled with fatherly duties for which Chad had seemed to be relieved. They had even laughed at his reaction. Sometimes Chad could be overly serious. She decided it might be better to wait until after their one-year anniversary before suggesting Chad move in with them. Good thing she'd waited.

***

Once home, Becca took a quick look around the house. It took a few moments for her to determine that, yes, Chad had packed up his stuff. All of his toiletries had been removed from the bathroom. His side of the closet now contained nothing but empty plastic hangers.

Good, at least he wouldn't be packing up his stuff in front of Jeremy. She wasn't sure how her son would take the news of Chad's disappearing from their lives.

***

Becca closed her fist and touched it down on the dresser in frustration. She'd just realized she'd agreed to let Jeremy spend Christmas Day over at his dad's this year because she'd planned to spend Christmas Day with Chad. Normally, she and Jeremy spent Christmas Day together, but this year, Ted's parents were coming to visit from Paris and wanted to spend time with their only grandchild. Of course, Becca had agreed in a heartbeat. Jeremy loved his grandparents whom he called, Nanny and Pappy.

Chad and Becca had even planned to go shopping to buy matching pajamas and take a bunch of selfies together. The tears started up again. Becca wiped them away. Life wasn't fair. That's what her father always said anyway. It sure felt true in the present moment. Becca's mom had died before she had started high school and her father had died from a heart attack the day after Jeremy was born. At least he'd had the chance to meet and hold Jeremy once.

Love sucks. Life sucks.

3

THE NEXT FEW DAYS DRAGGED ON. Almost another week went by before Jeremy asked about Chad, saying he hadn't see him in a long time. He seemed worried and asked if Chad was okay. Becca didn't know what to say. She wasn't ready to deal with it yet. Everything had happened so quickly. Jeremy looked directly into her eyes and asked if she was sure Chad was okay.

Sometimes kids are too smart for their own good.

Becca decided the best plan would be to change the subject. She told Jeremy he could pick out whatever he wanted for supper, including take-out.

His eyes opened wide with surprise. It didn't take him long to make his choice. He yelled while pumping his right hand up in the air. "Cheeseburger pizza! Cheeseburger pizza!"

Becca wasn't surprised. This cheeseburger pizza kick had been going strong over the last three months and it didn't look like it was going to let up any time soon. At this point, she was willing to do almost anything to avoid the topic of Chad. This way, she wouldn't have to cook, either. It was a win for both of them. She used the app on her phone to place the pizza order then quickly changed into sweats before scrounging around in the kitchen until she found the paper plates so they wouldn't have to do dishes.

As Becca walked by the living room, she wondered where they should put the Christmas tree. Should it go in the same spot as the year before or should they change things up? It was only the middle of November so she had plenty of time to decide so she went back to the kitchen where Jeremy stood, munching on something.

"What are you eating?"

"A mini Kit-Kat bar." He swallowed quietly.

"What did I tell you about your Halloween candy?" She locked eyes with her son.

"Um. To ask first?"

"If I catch you doing it again, all of the candy will have to stay in the kitchen. Understood?" She pointed to a cupboard.

"Yes, Mom." He turned and walked away.

Twenty minutes later, while Becca was in the middle of reading an email from work, there was a knock at the door.

She barely looked up from her laptop. "Pizza's here. Just grab it. It's already paid for."

Becca had been so engrossed in the email that it took her a moment to realize something was off.

Jeremy was whooping and hollering about something. Her instincts told her this had absolutely nothing to do with pizza.

Then she heard another voice, a familiar one. *No. It can't be.* But it was.

Him.

Becca quickly got up from the kitchen table and made her way to the front entrance where Chad stood beside Jeremy who was clinging to a fluffy black and white kitten. She put her hands on her hips and shook her head. This could not be happening. It was supposed to be over between them.

"Look what Chad brought me!" Jeremy almost shouted. "It's an early Christmas present. Chad said Santa can't bring the cat with him on Christmas Eve because it would scare the reindeer!"

Jeremy lifted it up and shoved it directly into her face.

Becca pasted on a smile. *Well this was interesting for sure.* Nothing like showing up with a cute present for Jeremy to try to win her back. What irritated her the most was that Chad and Becca had actually discussed the idea of getting a kitten for Jeremy *together*, as a joint present from both of them. Jeremy had been fascinated with cats for a long time. He was always reading facts to her about them whenever he got the chance. She didn't think he was capable of looking after a dog, but would be fine with a cat.

"Okay, so now we need stuff for the kitten and it needs a name." Becca looked at Chad pointedly. There was another knock at the door.

Chad looked at Becca inquisitively.

"Relax. It's the pizza we ordered for supper." Becca raised an eyebrow. They had broken up barely a month before and Chad already thought she'd moved on?

She opened the door and grabbed the pizza. Jeremy was already in the living room. Chad's eyes locked with Becca's. He didn't say a word. It was probably better that way.

She didn't know what to do. She didn't want to make a scene in front of Jeremy. Obviously, she had to talk to Chad, though. It wasn't okay to show up whenever he wanted. That wasn't how breakups worked. It was over. They definitely needed to talk. Chad smiled. Becca wanted to smack the smile off his handsome face. There was no way his perfect smile and charm were going to work magic this time around. What was done, was done. There was no turning back. Becca shook her head as she tried to shake off a sense of déjà vu.

Jeremy still hadn't put the kitten down. He looked so happy. Of course, she was going to let him keep the kitten. She wouldn't do that to him. It would break his heart. Plus, she had planned to get him a kitten for Christmas anyway. One less thing for her to do, but now Chad was the cool one, not her. She would have to figure something else out.

"Jeremy, you are going to have to put the kitten down so you can eat supper. Just put it on the floor and let it walk around. Wash your hands before you eat." Becca opened the pizza box and took out two slices and put them on a paper plate. "Sit and eat."

The kitten slowly walked around, inspecting its new environment.

Becca figured she'd get Jeremy fed and focused on the kitten in the living room while she and Chad would have a wee chat in the kitchen. She hoped they could talk quickly, quietly, and that Jeremy would be none the wiser. It sounded foolproof to her.

Becca looked up at Chad and offered politely, "Since you're here, would you care for a couple slices of pizza?" There was no need to be rude.

"Yeah, if you don't mind." Chad smiled. "I actually thought you might be upset."

Becca didn't reply. She took a slice of pizza out of the box, tossed it on a plate and handed it to him.

Chad sat down and started in. He seemed hungry, or maybe he was stalling for time in order to figure out the right words.

That's where he's wrong, Becca thought. *There are no right words anymore.*

From the living room, Jeremy called out. "Mom. It's going to need stuff, eh? Chad? Is it a boy or a girl?" He didn't look up, he was too busy with his new pet.

"It's actually a boy. Just a baby. He's ten weeks old. No worries about the stuff, kid. I brought it with me. It's in the car. I wanted both hands free to bring the kitten in. He's so little, I didn't want to drop him"

Trying to be casual, Becca asked, "What did you pick up for the kitten?" Chad was probably trying to win her back. It wasn't going to happen. She had to admit, she did miss the sex but that was honestly it. She had gone to her doctor and had tests done to make sure he hadn't given her anything else besides temporary heartache.

"I brought a food bowl, water bowl, small scratching post, a bag of food, a collar, cat litter and a scooper." Chad smiled. "I think he has enough to get him started."

Becca raised her eyebrows and shook her head. Chad had never been this organized before. He wasn't fooling anyone. She knew it was all an act. If only he knew he was wasting his time.

Damn him, he did have a gorgeous smile though. It was what had attracted her in the first place. She looked away. She needed to stay focused. Just because he was great to look at and amazing in bed, it wasn't enough to make things work. He had betrayed her. Their future was over before it even really got started.

"A collar?" Jeremy shoved the remaining bite of pizza into his mouth and ran into the kitchen, kitten in hand. "Let me put it on him!"

"Yeah, just a second. Let me finish eating and I'll get the stuff." Chad ruffled Jeremy's hair.

Becca stopped in mid-chew. Since when did Chad ever ruffle Jeremy's hair? Wow. He was really pulling out all the stops. Becca sucked in a huge breath and silently counted to ten. She tried not to laugh at the ridiculousness of his act. She really had to get him out of the house.

***

Chad brought loaded bags in from his car and set everything down in the living room. He took each item out of its bag, handing the black collar with the tiny bell to Jeremy.

"Wow. This is neat. It's going to look so cool!" Jeremy practically had to sit on the poor kitten to put the collar on. His entire face was lit up with excitement.

Becca quickly intervened, taking the kitten from Jeremy.

"Here, let me help you with that." The last thing she needed was for Jeremy to accidentally hurt him and her ending up with a damn vet bill.

"What are you going to name him?" Chad asked.

"I don't know yet." Jeremy said as he poured cat food into the dish with careful concentration.

"What about Boxer? Look at his eyes," Chad pointed. "He has a black circle around his left eye, like he was in a fight or something." The kitten was mostly white but did have a few patches of black all over.

Becca handed the kitten back to her son. She had to admit the kitten was cute.

Jeremy stroked the kitten for several moments, obviously thinking about the name. "I like that name. Boxer. Yep. Mom. I'm going to call him Boxer. Is that okay?"

"You can name him whatever you want. And it looks like Boxer is all equipped with everything he needs. Now I think maybe you and he should spend some time getting to know each other. Yes? Maybe together on the couch? Remember, this is all new to Boxer. Chad and I are going to be in the kitchen having coffee."

Becca motioned Chad to follow her.

4

ONCE IN THE KITCHEN, Becca started making the coffee.

Becca got straight to the point. "What's going on?" She had no desire for idle chatter.

Chad pulled up a chair. "I know you're upset. Just hear me out." He placed his hands on the table.

It was her house, she would speak first. After all, he had shown up uninvited.

"First the kitten. That was low. Jeremy doesn't even know about our breakup so I'm not sure why you're trying to win him over. It was supposed to be a Christmas gift. Now, no matter what I get, he won't care because he already has the kitten."

Chad smiled at this. Could Becca actually know what he was thinking right then? That he was smiling because at least he had accomplished something? That he'd been afraid Becca might tell Jeremy he couldn't keep the kitten then he'd be stuck with it? That there was no way he could've tried to return the kitten or pass him on to someone else? That he was just trying to figure out a way to get her to take him back? She knew he had an image to protect at all costs and Becca was the key to keeping everything in place. If what he had done ever became public, there was a possibility he could lose his job. He couldn't let that happen. He would do whatever it took. Did he actually believe that in time Becca would be his once again? That it would take only this one step? She would not come around. She would not, no matter how much he needed her to.

"I hope you realize the kitten doesn't change a thing," Becca said quietly. "It's still over between the two of us."

"Why? Why are you doing this? We get along so well and we've talked about moving in." Chad picked up his coffee as he spoke and took a sip. "I thought we were building something special."

"I told you, Chad. It's over. I can't... I'm nearing forty. I have Jeremy to think about. I don't want any complications."

"It's not complicated." Chad sounded defensive.

Becca shook her head. He should save his breath. She wasn't having any of it. "Don't even..." She took a frustrated breath. "Don't act like I decided to call it quits for no reason. That's not what happened, and you know it." She pointed a finger at Chad for emphasis. She took a deep breath. It was important she didn't raise her voice. The last thing she needed was for Jeremy to hear them arguing.

Chad appeared to be stalling for time. Becca watched as he took a last sip of coffee and got up to pour himself another. He motioned to see if she wanted more. She indicated she did.

"It was a one-time thing. I was just curious, really."

"Which would be fine had you satisfied your curiosity before we started dating and not while we were already sleeping together. I'm not going over this again. I asked and you confirmed it. We're done."

"I never meant for any of this to happen." Chad pleaded while Becca looked away. "Shawn doesn't mean anything to me. We can pick up where we left off."

He looked in the direction of the living room. He lowered his voice to make sure Jeremy wouldn't hear.

"We were both drunk. We'd had a couple of drinks at the bar.

We went back to his place. Zoey was away for a girls' weekend. Once there, we had a couple more beers. Shawn mentioned some porn site he'd seen and offered to show it to me. I said yes. Name one guy that would have said no to looking at porn."

She knew he was trying to justify his actions as if it was something all guys did. He paused, raised his eyebrows and appeared to wait for Becca to jump in or empathize. She met him with only silence, keeping her arms folded against her chest as she waited for him to continue. She knew there was more. She let him go on.

"We kept drinking and typing different word combinations into search engines. I have no idea what happened. Next thing I knew, we were in his bedroom and we started doing... I swear that was it." Chad shrugged. He stopped, obviously waiting for a reply.

Becca had heard enough. This conversation didn't change a thing. She kept playing the conversation she'd had with his friend, Shawn, over and over again. It hadn't been a one-time thing. The way Shawn had described it, they were in a relationship and Shawn didn't want to share Chad with her. This was kind of ironic since he was with Zoey and they were expecting a baby in the new year. The whole situation was one big mess that Becca certainly didn't want to be a part of.

Why was Chad trying to act like it wasn't a big deal? It was frustrating that he still wouldn't admit what had really been going on.

"Does Zoey know about the two you?" That was another question that had been bothering Becca. The last thing she wanted to do was run into Zoey and be blindsided. That wouldn't be good at all. They weren't close, they weren't even really friends, but still, the more information she had, the better she'd be able to handle whatever came next.

"No, of course not. Shawn doesn't want to lose her. Just like

I don't want to lose you. I can't. I'm sure if you give this some thought and time, we can work it out. I think maybe we both just need space for a bit."

Becca had to stifle a laugh. Nothing about this situation was funny but Chad appeared to be putting on some sort of act. She didn't even know who this man sitting across from her was. Now he was trying to make it seem like the whole thing had been mutual instead of the truth: Becca had dumped his ass.

"Look, it's over between us. I need for you to accept that and move on. Maybe you need to take some time and figure out your own sexual identity and what you want. I know what I want and it's not you." Becca turned her back on Chad and rinsed out her mug.

"I think he likes me, Mom. Boxer keeps licking me." Jeremy squealed from the living room.

"Awesome, maybe he can sleep with you tonight. It's almost bedtime so finish watching the movie."

Becca continued to putter around in the kitchen. She hoped that by not sitting back down, Chad would get the hint and leave.

5

BECCA'S MEMORY QUICKLY FLASHED back to the night she had ended things with Chad.

It had happened on the exact same day she'd received that mouth-dropping call from Shawn.

She and Chad had had supper plans so she'd let him come over as usual and prepared supper as if everything was fine. She had waited until they sat down to eat. She'd cooked Chad's favorite dish: lasagna. She took only one bite before asking him about his true relationship with his friend Shawn. When she'd used the word "relationship," she'd used air quotes.

Chad's eyes immediately locked with hers and his mouth actually fell open.

That was all it took for her to know, Shawn was telling the truth. At least to some degree. Obviously, she didn't know how far back their physical relationship went because, according to Chad, they'd been best friends since elementary school.

Surprisingly, they continued eating and talking like nothing had changed. Chad, seriously, had tried to convince Becca she was making something out of nothing and had never really got upset until he asked how she'd found out.

She decided to be honest with him. When Becca mentioned the phone call from Shawn, Chad had slammed his fist so hard on the table, the cutlery bounced off, landing with a clank-clank on the floor. After that, the conversation was over. They were over.

Except Chad kept sending texts. She'd ignored them for the most part. After a couple of weeks, she sent him a text saying he needed to pick up his belongings, and she gave him a time frame. If he didn't do so in the next forty-eight hours, she would make alternate arrangements.

When he asked about those alternate arrangements, Becca spelled it out for him clearly. She would throw his stuff into big garbage bags and drop them off at Shawn's house.

Now, here she was, facing him once again.

"Chad. You lied and you cheated. You have to figure things out on your own this time and I can't help you. I'm not sure you even know who you are anymore. Or what you want." Becca said all this while continuing to busy herself here and there around the kitchen.

***

He tried to grab her arm, realizing too late that that had definitely been a wrong move. A mistake. All he'd wanted was to patch things up. Couldn't she see that Shawn didn't mean anything to him? That it was only a way to blow off steam? Things couldn't really be over. They needed to have a future together. He'd had it all planned out.

He stood slowly and walked to the living room where he quickly patted the kitten, smiling and looking at Jeremy. "Good luck with Boxer, kid, I gotta go."

As he walked to the front door, she knew he was hoping she would stop him. Say something. She didn't. She knew he even stood outside the door in the cold as the first snow of the season started coming down. He remained there for what felt to her like forever, then he left. He had been defeated.

***

Becca had already decided that if she ran into Zoey, she wouldn't breathe a word of what she knew. It wasn't her place to tell her what was going on. If Zoey hadn't been pregnant, she might have said something, but the woman had already suffered one miscarriage. However, if Zoey wanted to ask her any questions directly, she felt she would have to be completely transparent.

As for Shawn, he seemed to be quite taken with Chad. Becca was betting that everything would eventually go up in flames. It was just a matter of time and she wanted no part of it. None of this was her fault. She counted her lucky stars that she'd found out before letting Chad move in.

6

A WEEK AFTER BOXER WAS WELCOMED into their family, a dozen long-stemmed yellow roses were delivered to Becca's work. Attached was a card from Chad saying he was sorry and wanted to start over again.

Becca didn't want to throw out the roses. They were pretty and roses were her favorite so she decided to hand them out to the girls at the youth center. When she saw their faces, she was glad she had. As a teen-aged girl, it wasn't often you received flowers, especially roses. It made them giggle, it made them smile and it gave them a moment to forget some of their troubles. It was the simple things that always made Becca feel good. Becca needed more feel-good moments, laughter and a whole lot less drama.

The same day the roses were delivered, Jeremy asked about Chad. He pointed out that he hadn't seen Chad in a while and asked what happened to him. Becca decided it was time to sit her son down and explain that things hadn't worked out and that they wouldn't be seeing Chad anymore. She explained that not all friendships worked out, that sometimes you were friends with someone for a while and then, for whatever reason, you just weren't friends anymore.

Jeremy shrugged it off and didn't seem too upset that Chad

was gone. His main concern seemed to be if he would get to keep Boxer. Becca assured him that Boxer was his to keep for good, no matter what. Again, she felt grateful that she hadn't let Chad move in with them. She and Chad were finally on the same page: no longer an item. Now that Jeremy knew it was over, it was time for everyone to move on.

After Jeremy went to bed that night, Becca worked on a list of things that needed to be done before the holidays. They already had an artificial tree, but she remembered that last year she'd decided to get more decorations. They definitely needed more garland, and she needed to start looking for stocking stuffers. Now that they had Boxer, maybe she would pick up a stocking for the kitten. She wrote it all down. Yes, she would do that and not say a word about it to Jeremy. He would be surprised when he woke up and it would make his Christmas even more special. Well, Christmas Eve, she corrected herself. They would open their gifts first thing Christmas Eve morning. After Becca and Ted had split up, they'd sat Jeremy down and explained that Santa kept track of all the kids with mommies and daddies who didn't live together anymore and always went to both houses to make sure no children were ever forgotten.

Becca had worried that the first year away from Ted, Jeremy would be disappointed by not being able to be with both parents. In the end, Jeremy didn't seem to mind celebrating with each of them independently. That was good. During the days leading up to that Christmas, Becca had had more than one nightmare of Ted dragging Jeremy out of the house, kicking and screaming. That was the last thing she wanted. However, when the time came, Jeremy hugged her longer than usual but then turned to go like any other time he'd left to go for a visit with his dad.

Christmas was the worst time to be single. Some people said it was Valentine's Day, but Becca wholeheartedly disagreed. She'd been single on Valentine's Day before and it hadn't bothered her. It wasn't that Becca actually wanted to be with someone, it was that she was disappointed how things had ended with Chad. She wondered why she hadn't noticed that anything was wrong.

That was the hard part, not seeing any of it coming.

Becca had a good job, a wonderful son, and her life was great. All she had been looking for was someone to share it with. Having someone to share it all with would be the icing on the cake.

Becca received a few text messages from Chad after he'd dropped by with the kitten. All of which she ignored. At first, she was tempted to respond but managed to stop herself. There was no point in answering him, it would just be adding fuel to a fire she did not want to tend. There was nothing he could say that would fix things or make her feel better. She needed to leave it alone.

She made a note on her list to find something to do on Christmas Day so she wouldn't spend it moping around the house. An image of herself kept popping into her head of her drinking wine alone and blowing her nose with tissues as she watched mushy holiday specials about happily-ever-after couples. Becca couldn't let *that* happen. The key was to keep busy. Some day she would meet the right someone.

7

EACH DAY AFTER WORK, Becca would go shopping and one by one she would cross items off her list. This simple act helped to boost her mood and made her feel productive. She felt better when she was out in public. Even if there were crying babies, screaming children and long lineups. All of it helped Becca feel normal. Even if just for a moment. That was exactly how she wanted to feel: normal.

***

It was a Wednesday, during the first week of December, and Becca was at work debating when she and Jeremy should put up the Christmas tree. At the same time, she wondered if Boxer would be attracted to the tree. They would have to keep an eye on him. She hoped it wouldn't be an issue. Becca would have to remember to put any breakable ornaments on the top half of the tree, just in case.

She heard the ding of the center's front entry doors. She looked up, baffled to see Shawn and immediately dropped her pen.

Shawn quickly sauntered over to the front desk where Becca was now standing.

Shawn practically spat the words out. "You need to stay clear of Chad. He's dangerous."

Becca's eyebrows rose. This would fall into the category of odd, for sure. "It's over with him, Shawn. Whatever's going on between you two and Zoey, that's on you. It's none of my business so keep me out of it." She sat again and picked up her pen. The conversation was over.

"You don't understand." Shawn began pacing back and forth in front of Becca's desk. "We went out the other day and I'm pretty sure he put something in my drink. I think he tried to kill me."

Shawn had her attention now. What the hell was he talking about? This wasn't making any sense. "What? When did this happen?"

"The other night. I hadn't seen him for a few days, even though I asked him repeatedly to get together. I wanted to apologize for the phone call to you. I'm sorry you got hurt. But I'm not sorry I told you about Chad and me."

Pen in hand, Becca waited. "Okay, and…"

"Anyway, he kept ignoring me because he was pissed. Which I don't blame him for. I just thought you had a right to know. I admit it. I was jealous. As soon as Chad started dating you, he barely had time for me anymore. I had to do something. I was desperate. That's why I called you. Oh. I'm rambling on here. He sent me a text and invited me over to order in Chinese and watch a movie together. Of course I jumped at the chance."

"Have a seat, Shawn. I can't leave the front desk right now, so we need to talk here. Do you want a cup of coffee or something?"

Shawn was looking more frazzled than she'd ever seen him. "That'd be great. Thanks." He sat in the closest chair.

Becca looked up as the coffee teased down from the Keurig to see the front doors open once again. It was a delivery man she'd never seen before. The regular guy must have been off sick.

"Cheerio, looks like donations of extra supplies for the center."

She quickly put the creamer carton and container of sugar on the desk beside Shawn and motioned for him to help himself. She walked over to the delivery man.

Rogan was what his name tag said.

"Thanks."

"There's more. I'll be right back."

Becca returned to the desk and watched as Shawn took a couple sips of coffee.

"Whatever he put in my drink, it knocked me out. I'm telling you he tried to kill me. I was out until the next day. I have no idea what happened. Oh my god, maybe he took videos or pictures of us doing something." Shawn was working himself up into quite the state. "Oh my god. What if Zoey finds out? What if he posts them on the Internet?"

The front doors opened again. Becca almost didn't look up because she figured it was the delivery man returning, but her training had taught her to always be sure.

It definitely was not the delivery man.

Chad stormed into the center, stopping in his tracks when he saw Shawn who immediately stood up.

Becca didn't move. This wasn't good.

Rogan entered once more and slowly unloaded the boxes. Was he watching the scenario? What was taking him so long? It wasn't like there was precious cargo in them or anything. Then again, maybe it was better to have someone else in the center now that both Chad and Shawn were facing each other, creating a potentially explosive situation.

Chad glared at Shawn. "What the hell are you doing here?"

"Telling her to stay away from you." Shawn's energy seemed to be slowly draining.

"You know what? You're the one needs to stay away from

her. Or else!" Chad took a few steps to close in on Shawn.

From the corner of Becca's eye, she could see Rogan standing there pretending that he was doing something instead of just watching events unfold.

Then Shawn seemed to catch a second wind. "Or else what? You going to try to drug me or kill me again? Or maybe both?"

Chad took another step forward and repeatedly poked his index finger into Shawn's chest. "I said stay away or you will damn well regret it."

Shawn clenched his hand into a fist and swung at Chad.

Rogan seemed to appear out of nowhere and quickly grabbed Chad's arms and folded them behind his back.

Chad tried to get away from Rogan's grip, but it was useless.

"Who is the big man now?" Shawn smiled, enjoying the moment, egging him on.

"I promise you. You will regret this!" Chad yelled.

Rogan kept Chad's arms fastened to his back while leading him out the front doors of the center.

Becca and Shawn stared at each other and waited.

***

Moments later, Rogan returned. "Everything okay here?"

"Yes. Um," said Becca. "Thanks for helping out. That could've turned really nasty."

"No worries." Rogan's ice blue eyes locked with Becca's.

It wasn't until Shawn cleared his throat twice, that she became aware she was staring at Rogan, taking him all in. She turned away. "Can I offer you a cup of coffee?"

She pulled out the selection of coffee pods and showed them to Rogan.

He selected a Hazelnut flavored pod from Starbucks.

She immediately popped it into the Keurig. "Shawn, did you want another cup before heading out?"

"Nah. That's okay. I better get home and check on Zoey."

"Shawn is it?"

Shawn nodded.

"You should be good to go," said Rogan. "I watched to make sure that asshole left the parking lot. The coast is clear."

"Thanks, mate." Shawn held out his hand to shake Rogan's, then left the center.

8

ROGAN STIRRED CREAMER into the coffee. "Okay, so do you want to talk about it or not?"

"Don't you have to get back to work or something?"

"Nope. This was my last drop off for the day."

This guy, Rogan, was a complete stranger—a complete stranger who had interfered and prevented a full-on brawl between Chad and Shawn. Imagine if a huge fist fight had taken place and she'd had to call the police? The police would have been surprised to find two adult males fighting instead of the normal call for one or two of her young clients.

She made a cup of coffee for herself.

"You don't have to if you don't want to, no pressure." Rogan took a sip of his coffee.

She was the only staff on duty right now. What if Chad came back? She'd never seen him behave like that. Clearly, there was an entirely different side to him, a side she didn't ever want to see again. She wasn't comfortable being alone even though she was wearing the mandatory panic button all staff wore, but it wasn't the same as having someone inside the center right here with her. It helped that it was a man who was easy to look at.

"One big mess that I hope is over. That's the best way to describe it."

"Sounded like some sort of love triangle."

"Chad, the guy you threw out of the center—thanks for that by the way—is my ex. We dated for a few months. Then one day, out of the blue, I receive a phone call from Shawn, the guy who was already here when you first arrived. He tells me he and Chad are lovers. Not only that, but it's been going on for a while. To top it off, Shawn has a fiancee named Zoey, and they're expecting a baby in the new year." Becca caught her breath and went back to sipping coffee. That was a lot of information to spill out at once.

"No shit," said Rogan, face without expression. "That's royally messed up. I take it Chad isn't taking the breakup well?"

Jet-black hair, ice-blue eyes, fit, maybe six foot, about her age or older. A woman could get lost in those eyes of his. She cleared her head. Her mind was wandering off. She had to stay in the present. "What about you?" she asked.

"I don't know what you mean."

"I watched you from the corner of my eye. You could've just unloaded the boxes and left but you didn't. You stayed. Why?"

Now the smile. "I needed you to sign this form and I had to be sure you were, in fact, Becca Thistle." He pulled out a folded piece of paper from his back pocket and handed it over to her.

She quickly unfolded it. It was nothing but a slip of inventory paper that did require her signature. She snatched up a pen, signed it and pushed the paper back across the counter toward him.

"Done," he said.

That smile. Those eyes.

"Mission completed."

"Have you always been a delivery man or were you someone else in a past life?" Becca teased.

"Actually, I used to be a cop."

***

That night Becca had a bad dream. She woke abruptly at 3:30 AM and could not get back to sleep, unable to shake the awful dream from her mind. Chad was flirting with Rogan, and Shawn had caught them together. She woke when, in the dream, she heard the sound of gun shots. After several unsuccessful hours of trying, she couldn't fall back to sleep. It was going to be a long day.

***

At work that morning, it was all Becca could do to stay awake. She normally limited herself to one cup of coffee a day, but she'd have to make an exception today. There was no way she could leave work early, either: she had to make sure all the boxes were ticked on her to-do list for the catered Christmas dinner. Then she had to start making a plan of attack for the scheduled renovations that were to start early in the new year. There was so much to do. Preparation was the key so she wouldn't become overwhelmed.

The bell at the center's entry door dinged and she looked up to see Rogan coming in with two boxes on a dolly. He was definitely a sight for sore eyes *this* morning. Not having had enough coffee must be why she was even thinking like this. It wasn't like her at all. *That smile.*

"Morning, Miss."

Becca stayed behind the front desk. "Morning."

The entrance bell dinged again. This time, both Rogan and Becca turned toward the sound.

In walked Chad, straight up to the front desk. "Morning, Becca. I brought your favorite, a caramel apple spice with whipped cream. From Starbucks." He seemed to be so focused on Becca, that at first, he didn't see Rogan.

"You didn't have to do that."

"But I wanted to."

Rogan jumped in with, "Where do you want me to put

the paint, ma'am?"

Chad's face went a shade paler. It took him only a split second to recognize Rogan.

"Same place as the other supplies, if you don't mind. We're starting renovations shortly, so I'll be using the paint very soon."

When Rogan grabbed the dolly to move it, she noticed he wasn't wearing a wedding ring and there was no sign that one had been worn anytime recently. She shook her head. *Why does that even matter?*

"Okay, will do." Rogan very slowly moved down the hallway with the boxes on the dolly.

9

BECCA TOOK A SIP FROM THE CUP of coffee that Chad had brought to her. She had to admit, it *was* delicious. It was one of her favorite drinks. Starbucks only carried it during the winter months during a brief window of time then it disappeared until the following year. The drink was good but packed a lot of sugar. *Good, that's something I definitely need today.*

Chad watched her savor the drink like a tiger hunting for prey. "I was wondering if we could get together for coffee over the weekend. You know. Just to hang out as friends."

His smile was gone. He actually looked sad. Becca wasn't going to fall for it. It was done. It was over between them. There was no way he was going to persuade her to have coffee with him. Especially since she'd seen his darker side during that episode involving Shawn. It would only lead to trouble. She didn't trust him for a single second. She held up the cup. "Bringing me my favorite drink from Starbucks, doesn't change a thing. It's over."

"No!" Chad slammed his fist on the front desk hard enough to make Becca jump and she spilled her coffee all over the desk.

She reached into her left pocket, feeling for the panic button she kept for safekeeping. If she pressed it, the police would arrive within minutes. In the last few years, Becca had only ever used it twice. Not once did she ever think she might need to use it on a fellow co-worker or an ex.

Just then, Rogan appeared. In the right place at the right time again. "Everything okay here?" Rogan looked from Becca to Chad and back.

Chad's eyes widened. Becca guessed that Chad was wondering why Rogan was so concerned since this had nothing to do with him. Were they not just having a conversation? It seemed he had already forgotten about his loud fist slam on her desk.

"We're talking. It's none of your business." Chad pointed toward the door.

Becca still had her finger on the panic button.

Rogan looked pointedly at Becca. "Tell me to go and I will go."

This was getting awkward. She wasn't sure what to say or do. The last thing she wanted was either one of them hanging around but if they both left at the same time, who knew what could happen in the parking lot. She was currently the only staff member on site. This meant she couldn't rush outside if the two macho men suddenly got into a fist fight. She pulled out paper towels and started to clean up the mess from her Starbucks.

She turned toward Chad. "I will see you next time work requires you to come to the center. Take care of yourself."

Chad stood there. Becca knew he was weighing the situation. He would have to continue coming to the center to see his clients. He needed to make sure he didn't ruin his reputation. He left quietly.

Rogan came closer to the desk which was when Becca noticed how good he smelled. Something mixed with coconut. She couldn't place it, but the aroma brought her comfort.

Rogan pulled a rag out of his pocket to help soak up the mess. "You okay?"

Becca was more upset about spilling the caramel apple cider

than she was about the ruined papers but she wasn't going to tell him that. She had counted on that spilled drink to help her get through the day.

Rogan wiped his hands on the rag, stuffed it back into his pocket and left.

Becca composed herself. She straightened up the desk and got back to work. She needed something to take her mind off things. *Maybe tonight will be a good night to put the tree up with Jeremy and Boxer.*

***

To kick off the evening, Becca ordered a cheeseburger pizza and after their stomachs were filled, Jeremy helped bring the Christmas tree and decorations out of the storage room. As they decorated the tree, *Rudolph the Red Nose Reindeer* played on the TV as did *Frosty the Snowman*. After the tree was decorated, they hung garland and moved on to deal with Christmas cookies. To make things quicker and a lot easier for them, Becca had bought pre-made gingerbread men. The cookies needed only to be decorated.

While they watched the movie, *A Christmas Story*, one of Jeremy's favorites, they drank homemade hot chocolate with whipped cream and decorated the cookies. The whole evening played out like a scene from a holiday movie and Becca went to bed counting her blessings that night. She was grateful her cell phone had not pinged with any messages from Chad.

10

THE WEEK BEFORE CHRISTMAS, Becca found herself actually humming at work. Things were going well. Boxer had not yet been able to take down the tree. Fingers crossed that it stayed that way. He had made a couple of attempts, but his size was against him. Becca was sure the tree was safe for this year; however, next year might be a different story. She would not worry about it until the time came.

Becca hadn't heard from Chad. This was good. She hoped this meant he was ready to leave her alone and move on with his life. She just wanted to forget about the whole thing. She needed to get through the challenge of the next few weeks. She still hadn't decided how she was going to spend Christmas Day after Ted picked up Jeremy. She didn't want to be all alone in the house.

Becca looked at her watch. For the first time that year, she had decided to go into work an hour later than usual. She hadn't worried because she knew Jean, a co-worker, could handle things. She had decided to use the extra time that morning to have a relaxing soak in raspberry bubble bath. As Becca approached the front desk at work, Jean clapped her hands, excited. Jean was brimming with glee, wanting to tell her something.

"Aren't we popular!"

"You're going to have to give me a little more than that to go on." Becca placed her purse under the desk.

Jean set a Starbucks cup in front of Becca.

"What's this?"

"It's for you. That's what."

"What do you mean this is for me?" Becca looked around. Chad had better not be hiding in the center somewhere. She was so done with that crap.

"It's your favorite. Caramel apple cider with whipped cream."

"Okay. Thanks for thinking of me this morning." Becca took a sip. It was still warm and as always, delicious.

"Oh, it's not from me. I think someone else was thinking of you." Jean smiled.

Becca took another sip then her mood quickly soured. "Only two people know I like this drink. You and Chad. I'll kill him."

Jean was shaking her head vigorously from side to side. "It wasn't me and it wasn't Chad." She clapped again, bursting with excitement.

Becca was in no rush so she decided to play along. She took another sip. She was bracing herself in case Chad suddenly appeared. Maybe even with flowers or chocolate to ask her out again. She was ready. This time she would walk him right out the door herself. Or call the police. Maybe if they spoke to him, he would tone things down. Enough was enough.

"Okay, it wasn't you, it wasn't Chad. So… Who's the mystery person who knows my favorite drink and dropped it off here at the center?"

"He said his name's Rogan. Girl, you have some 'splainin' to do."

Rogan's name was the last one Becca would have expected to hear. She thought maybe one of their young clients had surprised her with the drink. "Maybe you should start from the beginning."

"He was here like fifteen minutes before you walked in. Said he had a drink for you, even said your name. Said his name was Rogan. He wasn't wearing a uniform or anything but said he knew you. He's handsome. Such piercing blue eyes. I didn't see a wedding ring either." When she said the last part, Jean wiggled her eyebrows up and down playfully.

Becca laughed. And it felt good.

"Okay. I'll explain. But really, there isn't much, Jean." Becca began to tell Jean about the confrontation and Rogan's coming to the rescue while she worked on her caramel apple cider.

No sooner had Becca finished telling Jean all about Rogan, when the center doors opened and in walked a pair of police officers.

11

THIS ISN'T GOOD, Becca thought. She just knew that whatever was about to happen involved either Chad or Shawn.

"We are looking for a woman named Becca Thistle." A police officer, the name Milton printed on his badge, looked from Becca to Jean.

"I'm Becca. May I ask what this is about?"

The other police officer spoke up. "It's regarding a man named Shawn Aspen. Have you had any contact with him in the last few weeks?"

"Yes, why?"

"Can you tell us what took place the last time you saw him?"

"Is he okay?" Shivers filled Becca's entire body.

Milton responded. "I'm not sure how well you knew Mister Aspen, but he was found deceased yesterday afternoon. At the present time, his death is being treated as suspicious. We understand you were a witness to an argument that occurred right here recently."

The officer bent to glance at his notes, then continued.

"The incident was apparently between a Mister Shawn Aspen and a gentleman named Chad Doyle. According to the information we have, you were here as well as another man who was wearing a janitor-type uniform.

Becca was ready to collapse. Jean placed a chair behind her. "Take your time and start from the beginning."

***

It took nearly two hours before the police were satisfied with the information Becca provided. Jean had nothing to offer. They had asked more than once if Becca knew who this Rogan fellow was and how they could find him. She told them he delivered supplies to the center for the city. Then she remembered that he'd told her he had once been a cop. She told them everything she could. Apparently, Shawn's wife, Zoey, was convinced someone had killed him. They were waiting for an autopsy report. Becca wondered if Chad was really capable of harming another human being.

***

The next day Rogan walked into the center.

"What do we have here?" Becca asked, tentative, but managing a smile. It felt good. It had been a long time since the sight of anyone other than her son had made her smile. And since Rogan was so pleasant to look at, it was enough to make any woman smile.

"More cleaning supplies and one special delivery."

"A special delivery? What is it? All we're expecting are the cleaning supplies." Becca came around from behind the counter to check the boxes. Maybe there'd been a mistake. It happened from time to time. Suppliers were always getting all the different centers confused.

Rogan checked the list and scrolled down. "The cleaning supplies and two boxes of hats and gloves."

"If that's the case, it's a huge help and most welcome. We always need winter gear to give out to our clients." Things were starting to look up.

Some of the young people would refuse them at first, but after a couple of weeks, they would usually give in and come to her in the hope there were some left. She understood. Fashion was more important than comfort. But only to a certain point.

"Did you want me to open the boxes just to be sure?" Rogan asked.

"If you don't mind, that'd be great."

"Sure, anything you want." Rogan used a utility knife to slice open the top of the box. Then he lifted the lid and reached in to pull out a handful of hats in a variety of colors. "There you go, just harmless hats and gloves. Were you expecting something more sinister?"

She felt better knowing what was inside the boxes. After hearing about Shawn's death, she couldn't be too careful. "I just wanted to make sure they weren't a mistake. We often receive stuff that isn't meant for us. Sometimes, too, what's marked on the box isn't what's actually inside it." Becca leaned over to check the address label. She closed her eyes for a second to steady herself. She hadn't expected him to smell so good. *That trace of coconut!* She wanted to keep inhaling him. What was wrong with her?

Rogan interrupted. "So everything's good to go? I can unload the boxes now?"

"That'd be great. You can put them against the wall and I'll ask some of our young clients to move them to the storage room." Becca moved back behind the counter.

"Are you sure? I can bring them. The boxes are already on the dolly so really, it's no trouble at all."

His smile seemed genuine, not like Chad's phony million-dollar one. Right from the beginning, she'd thought Chad used that smile to get whatever he wanted, no matter the cost to everyone else. It had taken Becca too long to see all the signs, but Chad was nothing but a narcissist. He used people and once he didn't need them, he tossed them aside like garbage. To him, it was all about image.

"If you really don't mind, I'd appreciate it." Becca left the front desk to show him the way to the storage room.

The supply room was currently full, so overflow had to go inside the storage room. The center had been stocking up with enough supplies to last through the holidays. The hallway took a right turn then Becca unlocked the third door on the left and stepped aside.

12

BECCA WATCHED AS ROGAN EFFORTLESSLY stacked the boxes.

"What about the boxes with the hats and gloves," he asked. "Did you want those in here as well?"

"Actually, we can put them in my office for easy access."

Rogan helped bring the boxes to her office.

"Did the police contact you?" she asked him. She thought maybe he'd have mentioned it by now but hadn't. She needed to know.

"They contacted me. I told them everything I knew."

Becca apologized for his being dragged into the situation and added that she wasn't sure what had actually gone down.

Rogan told her not to worry about it. "It sounds like they still have things to look into. I did ask a buddy of mine who still works down at the precinct about it. Apparently, Shawn's wife, Zoey, had been at a doctor's appointment. He was supposed to go with her but at the last minute said something came up. She went to the appointment alone while Shawn went to work… Or so she thought."

"You want a coffee?" Becca asked. It didn't seem like the conversation was going to end anytime soon. Plus, she enjoyed being in his company. She felt secure and he made her smile. It seemed like he always knew the right thing to say and do. She appreciated that about him.

"That sounds perfect."

That smile again. She popped in a coffee pod.

Jared, one of the center's youth, walked by the front desk and tossed the mail. He looked at her then at Rogan and wiggled his eyebrows up and down at Becca.

This made her blush.

"Anyway, Zoey came home and found the door unlocked, which was unusual. She was expecting to find the house empty, with Shawn at work of course, but she noticed there were two used mugs sitting on the kitchen table, and half the batch of peanut butter cookies she'd made just that morning was gone. That's when Zoey started to wonder if Shawn really was at work like he'd said. She called the repair shop he worked at and they said he hadn't been at work all week. Apparently, he'd called in a few days previously asking for the week off, stating there'd been a death in the family and he had to go out of town." Rogan sipped his coffee.

"Poor Zoey. I can't even imagine."

"It gets worse," Rogan continued. "She went upstairs to lie down because she started feeling dizzy and nauseous. That's when she discovered Shawn's body."

Becca clamped her hand over her mouth. *Poor Zoey, how horrible!*

"Shawn was in bed, completely naked, and there was a used condom in the trash.

At first she thought he was just sleeping and started yelling at him. Then, when he didn't answer, she walked over to the bed and tapped him on the cheek. He didn't move. That's when she realized something was really wrong and called 9-1-1. That's all they've got for now."

"The whole situation is bizarre."

***

Later during their spaghetti supper, one of Becca's favorites, Jeremy asked if she'd gotten good news. She paused, wondering what he might be talking about.

"Not that I'm aware of, Jeremy. Why?" Did he know something she didn't?

"You're in a good mood, Mom. So did something nice happen today?"

Becca put down her fork and laughed. It felt good. She couldn't remember the last time she'd really laughed. Just months ago laughing had come easily, but now she didn't feel it often enough. Well, maybe it had lately… with Rogan around. Even though the day before had brought bad news about Shawn, Rogan had brightened this day by his presence.

"No. No good news. Just feeling better I guess and I'm getting excited about Christmas. Aren't you? Maybe you'll get a special present."

"Okay. I'm just glad you're happy." Jeremy stuffed pasta into his mouth so quickly, Becca had to warn him to slow down. She was always afraid he would choke on his food.

As she watched him, she had to admit that today had been a good day. She had finished the rest of her Christmas shopping for Jeremy. All she had left to do was wrap the presents which she would do the night before the big day. She had a tradition she'd started when she first met Ted and finally had someone to buy gifts for: she would buy a small bottle of rum and a large bottle of Coke. She would mix herself a drink to enjoy while she wrapped all the Christmas gifts in one go. She got the idea from her own mother who used to do the same thing every year. Becca found it extremely calming and Christmas was the only time she allowed herself to enjoy rum and Coke. She was good to go and on top of everything. *Good.*

13

BECCA DECIDED, THAT AFTER JEREMY HAD BEEN picked up by his father on Christmas morning, she would go in and spend the day at work. She didn't really need to as she had more than enough staff to cover the shift. She figured there was no way she would be able to mope around if she was at the center. It would be alive and bustling with the energy of all the young people. Some would be reuniting with their parents, some would be alone, and others would be indifferent. Either way, being present at the community center would make her feel alive and normal. Exactly what she wanted and needed. That was what the Christmas spirit was all about, feeling alive and grateful.

At the youth center, they would be having a nice, big catered dinner of turkey with all the festive trimmings. Becca could make herself a plate and bring it home to enjoy later on in the evening. Maybe then she would relax and sip on a single rum and Coke.

She pictured herself all curled up watching her favorite movie, *A Christmas Carol,* the one with Alistair Sims. Most of the other versions were good as well, but she'd always had a special love for this one. Maybe because it was the same version her own mother had favored. Ever since Becca could remember, her family would watch that movie. Her mother had always insisted because she herself hadn't grow up watching it, but an older sister had always read a chapter from the book by Charles Dickens every night leading up to Christmas Eve. On that night, the final chapter would be read.

Jeremy would be staying with his father until after supper on the 27th. Even if Becca had more than her usual to drink Christmas Eve, no worries, she would have the entire Boxing Day to rest and do nothing. She would take a soak in the tub—a bubble bath—and watch more movies later. Really, the sky was the limit!

***

A couple days later at work, Rogan showed up again with a delivery. "Hey, Miss. More boxes for you." *And there was that heartwarming smile.*

"Are you going to be the regular guy from now on?" The question was out of Becca's mouth before she could stop herself.

"I might be. Does it matter?"

That wasn't the answer Becca had expected. "I guess it doesn't."

"Nothing extra today. Just more paint supplies. Did you want me to put them in the storage room again?"

"If you don't mind." Becca headed to the storage room alongside him to unlock it.

As Becca returned to the front desk with Rogan trailing behind her, she stopped dead in her tracks. Chad was at the front desk.

Before she could say anything, he spoke. "Relax. I'm here on business." He said this with a glare in Rogan's direction.

"What do you need?" Becca folded her hands across her chest. He'd better be quick.

"I need to help Jared fill out that application we've been waiting for. Can we use your office? Should only take a half hour or so." Chad was speaking to Becca but his gaze remained on Rogan.

Chad had been waiting for a package with different rental applications and information on starter kits for some of the youth moving out on their own. Becca guessed Jared's package had arrived.

"Of course," she said then called Jared to the front desk.

She watched until Chad and Jared had made their way back to her office so wasn't aware that Rogan was waiting there, looking at her. "Do you want me to stay? I mean… I'm sure you can handle things on your own, but…"

Without a second thought she said, "That'd be great. I'll get the coffee."

As they chitchatted, Rogan talked about how he used to be a police officer but had left the force the year before and moved to Ottawa to be with his mother who was in long-term care. He was an only child. He wanted to make sure he was doing everything in his power to make sure she was looked after and comfortable.

She was just about to tell Rogan how sweet he was when the doors to the center opened and in walked a familiar face. Becca recognized Officer Milton immediately.

Rogan and Milton exchanged looks.

A second officer followed Milton in.

Something was wrong.

14

OFFICER MILTON SPOKE TO BECCA FIRST. "Have you had contact with Mister Doyle recently?" His eyes never moved from hers. He was definitely in serious mode.

"Actually, yes. Today."

After exchanging glances with a second officer. Milton continued, "Exactly what time was this?"

Becca glanced at Rogan.

He shrugged his shoulders.

The whole situation was getting stranger by the moment. "He's here," she said.

"You mean here right now? Inside this building?" Milton asked.

"In my office. With one of our young clients. He stopped by to help him with an application. That's part of his job. Working with the youth." Becca glanced around behind her. She wasn't sure what she was expecting, but she had a feeling something dramatic was about to happen.

The other officer stepped away and reached for a radio.

Becca's heart rate increased.

"All right," said Milton. "You two are to stay right here and I need to know where the rest of the youth are."

Becca quickly ran her finger down the sign-out board. She

figured there were only about five young people in the center at the moment, including Jared. "Five. Probably in the kitchen, dining room, living room. Maybe the bathroom."

"I need you to get everyone safely into one room and make sure they remain there. And how many youth are with Mister Doyle at the moment? Just the one?"

Becca nodded. Her feet were frozen to the floor.

"Gather the youth quickly and quietly then come back here."

Becca did as she was told. All four were in the living room. She asked Sam, the most reliable young lad, to start a video game contest. The prize would be a twenty-five-dollar gift card to Tim's for whoever came in first. She hoped that would keep them busy long enough. Once done, she returned to the front desk where Milton waited. "Four are in the living room. Well occupied and distracted I hope. Jared is with Chad."

Through the front door, Becca could see two police cars pull up out front, lights flashing.

"Okay," said Milton. "So there's one youth named Jared with Chad Doyle. No one else, correct?"

"Can you tell me what this is about? I'm responsible for all these youth. I need to make sure nothing happens to any of them. Including Jared. What's going on?"

She didn't want to overstep but at the same time, it was her center and all the young clients were her responsibility.

Rogan came up beside her and gently placed his hand on her shoulder. Immediately, she felt calmer but she now had a weird sense of butterflies floating around in her stomach. She wondered if it was because she'd skipped breakfast that morning. Or if it was from Rogan's touch. But now was not the time to be examining either possibility.

Milton spoke. It seemed to Becca that his cop voice was even deeper. What he said did nothing to comfort her. "We have a warrant for the arrest of Mister Doyle. We will remove him from the premises quickly and quietly."

This can't be happening!

Two more police officers entered the building, one male and one female. Now there were four.

Milton asked where her office was.

Becca led them down the hallway and pointed to her office door.

Milton motioned for her to go back.

She wasn't about to argue with him. She did as instructed and went directly to Rogan. Her hand brushed his. Their eyes met. She was shaking. She couldn't help it.

"You cold?" Rogan asked.

"Just nerves. I can't believe this is happening. I hope it all goes smoothly."

Rogan removed his flannel work jacket and laid it across her shoulders.

She looked up into his eyes and cuddled into the jacket. It felt good against her skin. It smelled like him.

"Want me to make you a coffee?"

She nodded.

15

BECCA HEARD CHAD'S VOICE of indignation before she actually saw him. "You can't do this to me. I haven't done anything wrong. You have no proof. You need to let me go right now. I want a lawyer!" Chad's voice was getting louder by the minute.

Three officers were escorting him out the door. She correctly assumed the other police officer was in the office with Jared.

"I demand to know what it is I'm being charged with. I want to know now." Chad had attempted to stop walking but the police officers just started dragging him.

"Murder. Do you need me to read you your rights again, Mister Doyle?" Milton was actually smiling at Chad.

"What the hell are you talking about? You can't prove anything!"

"We have an eyewitness that places you at the home of the Aspens around the time of the murder."

That seemed to shut Chad up. He didn't say a word after that as they led him out of the center.

***

The night Chad was arrested, Becca had the best sleep she'd had in months. She slept for nine hours straight. Not once did she wake up nor did any nightmares pull her in. The next morning, she felt well-rested and light in spirit. It was hard to describe but whatever it was, she was enjoying it and wanted it to last as long as possible. It was beginning to look like she'd be able to hold strong and make it through Christmas and the New Year. Time for change. Time to let go and accept the new opportunities the new year would offer. She was actually looking forward to it.

***

Ted picked up Jeremy at 11:00 AM on Christmas Day.

Before heading to work, Becca had lasagna, left over from the previous day's take-out. She was happy to have something ready to eat. Then it was off to work.

She arrived shortly before 3:00 PM. She dealt with some of the paperwork. She loved working at the center but often waited until the last minute to do the admin stuff. It wasn't exactly the most enjoyable part of the job. She preferred spending time actually interacting with the youth. That's where she felt she made the most difference.

The center was abuzz with youthful energy. She loved it. It made her feel alive, grateful for all that she had. She loved her job and she had her wonderful, healthy son. In the grand scheme of things, she'd already hit the jackpot. Did she really have the right to ask for anything more?

Maybe she did.

The turkey was set to be delivered by the caterers at 7:00 PM. There would be four different types of pie for dessert: apple, blueberry, lemon meringue and pecan. After supper, she would help wash the dishes and clean up. Then she planned to get a head start on the packing. Several of the rooms in the center were going to be renovated at the beginning of the new year. The first step was to paint them, so everything inside each room had to be packed up in boxes and labeled.

***

The center had been extremely busy all day with people coming and going with family visiting the youth. The door was opening and closing so often that most of the time, Becca barely felt the need to look up. However, she did as soon as she heard his familiar voice.

"Hey, Miss. I have more boxes for you."

That smile.

She couldn't help but smile back. "How did you get stuck working on Christmas Day?" He was the last person she expected to see on Christmas so was quite happy to see him. It brightened her day even more.

"I volunteered. Most of the other staff have families so would rather spend the day with them. The deliveries don't have to be done today, but they'll just keep piling up so I thought I'd see what I could get done." He paused, eyebrows up, those blue eyes piercing into hers, asking her why she was working on Christmas Day, too.

She could only think of his beautiful eyes so she shrugged.

He continued. "I honestly don't mind working. I'd rather be doing something to pass the time than be at home alone with nothing on TV but mushy holiday movies." The smile. "I already visited Mom. The staff said she wasn't feeling the best and was resting when I arrived. I stayed for an hour then told them to call me if she needed anything. Why are you working? Afraid Chad's going to escape from prison or something and you feel safer here?" Rogan laughed.

It was the first time she'd heard him laugh. She rather enjoyed the sound of it and wanted to hear him do it again.

"Well? What about yourself? There is no way you need to be here."

"I seem to be in the same situation as you." she said, pretending to look over the paper work in front of her.

"Not exactly in the same situation, but sort of intriguing."

"I guess."

"Are you going to tell me or make me guess?"

Becca stopped flipping the papers and looked up. She hadn't expected a reply. She figured he would unload the boxes and leave. "Well. My son Jeremy—he's almost eleven—is at his dad's. I didn't feel like being alone." Becca waited to see what kind of reply Rogan might come up with. This was the first time she'd ever mentioned her son. It didn't seem to matter.

"Do you want me to unload the boxes for you?" Rogan didn't appear ready to leave. Could he be unhappy spending the holidays alone?

"If you don't mind." *There it is,* she thought. *He's going to unload the boxes and be on his way and that'll be that.* Which was fine, but she still felt a sense of disappointment. Maybe at some point in the future she'd gather up the courage to ask him out for coffee or something. Maybe now was not the time, though.

After Rogan had placed the boxes in the storage room, Becca walked with him to the exit door instead of going behind her desk. "How many deliveries do you have left to do today?" She didn't want him going. Not yet. She was stalling and she didn't care.

"Actually, this is my last one. Looks like I'll have to find another way to occupy my time for the rest of the evening. Why do you ask?"

His eyes locked with hers. They sparkled. Then he actually winked at her. Butterflies returned to her stomach. She couldn't help but smile. "Have you had supper yet?"

"No. Why do you ask?"

"We'll be putting on a fancy turkey dinner here shortly and there will be more than enough. You're welcome to stay if you wish. No pressure. Just thought I'd offer." She shrugged as if she didn't care while feeling the complete opposite. She wanted him to stay. She wanted to be around him. He was nice to look at. He made her smile. She enjoyed talking with him. And he made her feel safe.

"That offer is very difficult to refuse," he said. "You sure nobody will mind?"

"Not me, for sure. It might be noisy. These young people have a lot of energy, especially during the holidays."

There. She'd given him a fair warning.

"Don't worry about me," he said. "Noise doesn't bother me at all. I'll be glad for the company. It's too quiet at my apartment."

16

SUPPER ARRIVED AN HOUR LATE but it didn't matter. Everything was perfect. Technically, the caterers weren't really late because as far back as Becca could remember, Christmas dinner had never arrived on time.

Each of the youth pitched in to help serve the meal. During dinner, Becca and Rogan made small talk but, for the most part, they kept busy and were entertained by the sounds of youthful enthusiasm. Some of the youth remained quiet while others shared memories of favorite Christmas toys they'd received from Santa as kids.

After dessert was served, strangely enough, most of the youth started taking off. Some went outside to smoke and others went for a walk. Apparently, they had more pressing matters to see to other than helping clean up after the dinner. Not that Becca was surprised. A couple of them settled in to watch movies. At first, three of them did stay to help but fifteen minutes later they left saying they had done their part, which was probably the truth. A good portion of the dishes still needed to be washed and dried.

Rogan saw the look on her face and laughed. "No worries, I'm handy in the kitchen. How about you wash and I dry? Like that saying: many hands make light work."

Becca turned and they locked eyes again. She couldn't believe he was offering to stay to help out. She appreciated the gesture. She handed him a dish towel printed with candy canes.

Rogan raised his eyebrows at it. "Cute."

It took them just over an hour to wash, dry, and put away everything. Becca had to admit she'd washed the dishes more slowly than normal. She enjoyed spending time with him. She didn't know what she was going to say or do once all the dishes were out of the way. She was stalling again. Was this going to become a habit of hers when she was around Rogan?

They talked the entire time. Rogan was two years older than she was, making him thirty-seven. He'd never been married and didn't have children. He'd been delivering for the same company for a year now. Before that, he'd been a police officer, but had relocated from Kingston to Ottawa to be with his mom in her final days. To do this, he arranged a leave of absence from the police force. With the different shifts and time required for staying at locations during situations and writing daily reports, he couldn't be a cop and be able to be there instantly for his mother when she needed him to be. Family was more important than anything.

Becca in turn told him about Jeremy and Ted. They agreed that the past was the past. That it was time to let go and enjoy the smaller moments, no matter if those moments led somewhere or not.

After the dishes were done, she expected Rogan to leave. If that were the case, she wasn't sure if she was going to be mentally able to stay alone and do the renovation-prep packing. She thought her time might be better spent at home replaying the evening over and over again in her mind.

"Is there anything else I can help out with? Are there any other chores? Please say yes."

"Really? Don't you want to go home and enjoy the rest

of the evening?"

"No. I'd rather be here. I mean, if that's okay with you."

They locked eyes.

"I don't mind at all. Next up on the agenda then is packing boxes. There's quite a bit to be done, but if I can get a head start, that'd be great. I appreciate all the help I can get."

Becca grabbed a stack of boxes, packing tape and a black marker and upstairs they went to put boxes together and pack up the first room.

When they finished each box, they sealed it with packing tape, wrote the room number and contents on it then stacked it outside the room, all the while chatting about different topics as the evening carried on.

Then Rogan stopped what he was doing. "Oh. It's after midnight. I didn't think it was that late."

"Time just flew by, didn't it?"

"Do you want to stop then?"

"To tell you the truth, I'm not sure."

Rogan laughed.

"What's so funny?"

"You realize we are literally packing boxes on Boxing Day?"

Becca couldn't help but laugh along with him. It was funny.

She didn't know what she wanted to happen next but she definitely didn't want whatever this was to stop. She had to be practical, though. It was time to call it a day. It sucked because she couldn't remember the last time she'd felt this good. She deserved to be happy, just like everyone else. That wasn't asking too much, was it? *No. It wasn't.*

17

BECCA HAD ALWAYS DONE THINGS by the book. She didn't believe in one-night stands and had always been careful. That was just her way. Tonight, she wanted to do things differently. This time, she was going to take a leap of faith and see where she landed. Maybe nowhere and that was okay. At least she would know. No more regrets or what ifs. She decided this one time she would be the one in control and make the first move.

"Look. I'm not sure what you want to do but I'm really enjoying your company."

"Me too. I don't want to seem too forward. To be honest, I don't know where we go from here. If anywhere."

"I don't normally do anything like this but do you want to come back to my place? To be clear, I don't want a one-night stand or anything. Maybe we can watch a not-so-mushy Christmas movie together? That way neither of us will have to be alone for the holidays." She took a breath, treading carefully to the edge of wherever she was going. She had dipped her toes in to test the waters.

"That does sound good but I need to know the name of the movie first before I can make such a life-changing decision."

Is he making a joke or is he seriously asking?

Becca let go of the breath she'd forgotten she was holding.

She couldn't believe it. She'd just asked him to her place. There was no turning back. Things would either go really well or really badly.

Of course now would be the time she started second guessing herself. For all she knew, he could be a serial killer. She immediately tried to push that thought from her mind. He worked for the City so had to have passed a police record check. And he'd been a police officer.

He could also be lying about everything.

She shook her head. Not tonight. She wouldn't allow her mind to go there. It was Christmas. Well. Boxing Day. It was the holidays. She deserved some joy and maybe one day soon she'd have the icing on her cake. Make that chocolate icing on her chocolate cake. *Any icing on any cake would be great.*

"For the record, the movie is called *A Christmas Carol*. It's actually a tradition for me. I watch it every year. I usually watch it on Christmas Eve or Christmas Day. I grew up watching it as a kid."

"That sounds great. It'll be nice to just be with someone and not be alone on a holiday."

"Let's make this the last box we pack up on Boxing Day and then be off to enjoy some time together," Becca said.

Before they left the empty room, Rogan walked over and pressed his lips down on Becca's. She closed her eyes, she wanted more. So much more, but she had to stop that line of thinking. She'd invited him back to her place to watch a movie. She had no intention of jumping him the second they walked through the door. *At least not tonight.*

"We should probably get going before the entire holiday is over." Rogan gestured toward the door.

In the parking lot, Rogan blew her a kiss as he was getting into his red pickup truck.

She laughed out loud. It echoed. She was happy.

***

Once settled in at her place, Becca poured them each a rum and Coke and started the movie.

An hour later, she was cuddled in Rogan's arms, her fingers interlaced with his.

Would this work out? She had no idea, but for now, it didn't matter. What mattered was, at this very moment, she felt good and had taken a leap of faith. Maybe she'd found her icing on the cake. Only time would tell. For now she was content in the moment and that was what mattered. Becca's past was boxed up and it was time for her to unpack a new set of adventures.

Acknowledgments

THERE ARE SO MANY STEPS to writing a book and it takes a team for everything to come together, to reach the point where the book is physically in my hands. I would like to say a special thank you to my editor, Phyllis Bohonis, who continues to take on my projects, tells it like it is, and provides encouragement when needed. This book wouldn't be here without the magical talent of my book designer, Sherrill Wark of Crowe Creations. Thanks for your never-ending patience and feedback.

A special thank you goes to my readers who keep in touch and always ask about my current projects.

About the Author

Catina Noble is an Ottawa writer with over two hundred publications including books, articles, short stories and poetry. Her work has appeared in many publications including *Chicken Soup for the Soul, Bywords, Woman's World Magazine, Perceptive Travel, The Mindful Word* and many others. Her poem "You Can't See Me" took first place in the Canadian Author's Association's National Capital Writing Contest in 2014. Four of her books have received the Reader's Favorite

Five Star Award: *Finding Evie*; *Vacancy at the Food Court and Other Short Stories*; *I'm Glad I Didn't Kill Myself*; and *Everest Base Camp: Close Call*. In 2006, Catina graduated from Algonquin College with her Social Services Worker Diploma and in 2009, she graduated from Carleton University with a Bachelor's Degree in Psychology. She works full time in her field, writes, and is currently enrolled in the Creative Writing Certificate and the Addictions & Mental Health Program at Algonquin College. Sometimes her dog, Aspen, supervises her creative writing process, but her favorite place to write is at a local coffee shop.

Other Books by Catina Noble

Bandages (2024, poetry, chapbook)

Teal, Teal Flint (2023, YA, trilogy)

Letter Rip (2022, textbook on writing)

Finding Evie (2022, fiction)

The Happily Ever After? (2022, poetry, chapbook)

El Camino on a Wrecked Ankle (2020, non-fiction)

Everest Base Camp: Close Call (2020, non-fiction)

Lost at 13 (2017, Cat's Journals)

Vacancy at the Food Court and Other Short Stories (2016, fiction)

I'm Glad I Didn't Kill Myself (2016, Cat's Journals)

Katzenjammer (2015, poetry)

Available in print and/or e-book from the Amazon dots and select fine book stores.